Moose!

Moose!

Robert Munsch

illustrated by
**Michael
Martchenko**

Scholastic Canada Ltd.
Toronto   New York   London   Auckland Sydney
Mexico City New Delhi Hong Kong Buenos Aires

The illustrations in this book were painted in watercolour
on Crescent illustration board.
The type is set in 18 point ITC Usherwood.

Scholastic Canada Ltd.
604 King Street West, Toronto, Ontario M5V 1E1, Canada

Scholastic Inc.
557 Broadway, New York, NY 10012, USA

Scholastic Australia Pty Limited
PO Box 579, Gosford, NSW 2250, Australia

Scholastic New Zealand Limited
Private Bag 94407, Botany, Manukau 2163, New Zealand

Scholastic Children's Books
Euston House, 24 Eversholt Street, London NW1 1DB, UK

www.scholastic.ca

Library and Archives Canada Cataloguing in Publication
Munsch, Robert N., 1945-
Moose! / Robert Munsch ; illustrated by Michael Martchenko.
ISBN 978-1-4431-0718-1
I. Martchenko, Michael II. Title.
PS8576.U575M57 2011a   jC813'.54   C2010-906029-6

14 13 12 11   Printed in Malaysia 108   15 16 17 18 19

To Luke Van Zutphen,
Cape Breton Island.
—R.M.

One Saturday morning Luke woke up very, very early. He got dressed, ate a bowl of cereal and went outside. There, standing by his tree house, was a large, enormous MOOSE.

Luke looked at it and yelled,

"MOOOOOSE!"

Then he ran around the yard three times and went inside to wake up his father.

His father was asleep like this:

ZZZZZ, ZZZZZ, ZZZZZ, ZZZZZ.

He had been on the computer till three in the morning.

Luke said very quietly, "Daddy!"

He didn't wake up.

Luke said a little louder, "DADDY!"

He still didn't wake up.

Luke yelled as loud as he could, "DAAAAAAAAAAADDY!"

He still didn't wake up, so Luke grabbed a pillow and whapped him on the head.

His father jumped out of bed and yelled:

"What's the matter?

"What's the matter?

"What's the matter?"

"Out by my tree house," said Luke, "is a large, enormous moose."

"That is crazy," said his father. "There is no moose out by your tree house. Moose do not come anywhere near the farm."

Still, he decided to go see what was going on. He got dressed, opened up the back door, stepped outside, rubbed his eyes, opened them up and yelled,

"MOOOOOSE!"

That frightened the moose and it jumped right up in the air and came down on him.

Luke's father said, "GWACKKKH!"

Luke said, "Daddy?"

Luke decided to go get his mother.

His mother was asleep like this:

ZZZZZ, ZZZZZ, ZZZZZ, ZZZZZ.

She had been watching TV till three in the morning.

Luke said very quietly, "Mommy!"

She didn't wake up.

Luke said a little louder, "MOMMY!"

She still didn't wake up.

Luke yelled as loud as he could, "MOOOOOOOMMY!"

She still didn't wake up, so Luke took off his hat and whapped her on the head.

His mother jumped out of bed and said:

"What's the matter?

"What's the matter?

"What's the matter?"

"Out by my tree house," said Luke, "is a large, enormous moose."

9

"Don't be ridiculous," said his mother. "There are no moose in our backyard. Moose do not come anywhere near the farm." Still, she decided to go see what was going on. She got dressed, opened up the back door,

10

stepped outside, rubbed her eyes, opened them up and yelled,

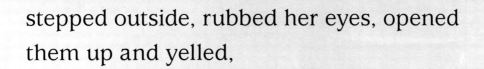

That frightened the moose and it jumped right up in the air and came down on her.

Luke's mother said, "GWACKKKH!"

Luke said, "Mommy?"

Luke wanted to get the moose off his mother. He sat down and thought for a while, and then he got an idea.

He ran into the kitchen, opened the refrigerator and got out three big, orange carrots. He held them out the door and said, "Here, moosie, moosie, moosie."

The moose came over and smelled one carrot: *sniff, sniff, sniff, sniff.*
It ate the carrot.

CRUNCH!

Luke said, "I think I like this moose."
The moose smelled another carrot: *sniff, sniff, sniff, sniff.*
The moose ate the carrot.

CRUNCH!

Luke said, "I want to keep him for a pet."
The moose smelled another carrot: *sniff, sniff, sniff, sniff.*
The moose ate the carrot.

CRUNCH!

Luke said, "He can live in my tree house!"

Just then his mother lifted her head and said, "Luke! Get me a broom."

"Do you mean a little broom for shooing away birdies?" said Luke.

"No!" said his mother.

"Do you mean a medium-sized broom for shooing away bunny rabbits?" said Luke.

"NO!" said his mother.

"You don't mean a LARGE, ENORMOUS BROOM for shooing away cute moosies?" said Luke.

"YES!" said his mother.

So Luke got the LARGE, ENORMOUS BROOM for shooing away cute moosies and gave it to his mom.

First Luke's mother chased the moose around the yard.

Then the moose chased Luke's mother around the yard.

Then the moose ate the broom.

"This is not working," said Luke.

"Luke!" said his father. "Get me a hose."

"Do you mean a little hose for chasing away birdies?" said Luke.

"No!" said his father.

"Do you mean a medium-sized hose for chasing away bunny rabbits?" said Luke.

"NO!" said his father.

"You don't mean a LARGE, ENORMOUS HOSE for chasing away cute moosies?" said Luke.

"YES!" said his father.

So Luke got the LARGE, ENORMOUS HOSE for chasing away cute moosies and gave it to his father.

First Luke's father chased the moose around the yard.

Then the moose chased Luke's father around the yard.

Then the moose took the hose and had a wonderful bath.

"This is not working," said Luke.

Then Luke's three sisters came out of the house. Each one was holding a large, enormous squirt gun for squirting cute moosies.

"That will not work," said Luke. "Moosies like water."

"Yes, it will work," said his sisters. "Watch!"

They walked into the middle of the yard and yelled, "HEY, MOOSIE!"

The moose turned around, saw the squirt guns and yelled, "HUNTERS!"

"That works," said Luke.

The moose ran into the kitchen, took some carrots out of the refrigerator, ran out the front door and did not come back.

"See!" said Luke's sisters.

Then they squirted Luke:

SKRONK! SKRONK! SKRONK!

and went back inside.

Luke said, "That was a cute moose. It can still live in my tree house."

And he took the rest of the carrots out of the refrigerator and ran after it.